Bibi

Jo Weaver

PEACHTREE
ATLANTA

On a still morning, the sun rose over the lake.
Bibi ruffled her feathers and opened an eye.
She had been with the flock for as long as anyone
could remember and was older than anyone knew.

Her name could often be heard amid the chatter on the lake.

"Bibi showed me how to preen my feathers."

"Bibi taught me how to stand on one leg."

Every flamingo recognized her call, as she guided them in a graceful dance on the glassy water.

When new parents were ready
to lay their eggs, Bibi led them away
from the edge of the lake. There on
the soft mud, she showed them how
to build nests for their chicks.

"Welcome to the flock, Toto," she
said, greeting the newest flamingo.

The chicks took their first steps here, growing stronger every day.
But as the sun beat down, the earth around them was drying up quickly.

"We can't stay here any longer," the flamingos agreed.
"There's no food, no shade . . ."

"No water!" said Bibi, turning toward the lake.

The water's edge had shrunk away, into the shadow of the distant volcano.
They could reach it quickly by air, but their chicks couldn't fly yet.

"I know the way by foot," said Bibi to the flamingos. "You fly ahead, and I'll walk with your chicks. We'll meet you by the shore."

"How do you know where to go?" the chicks asked Bibi anxiously.

"I made this journey when I was small like you.
I was afraid then too," she said.

As she spoke, she noticed a
small chick lagging behind.

It was Toto, collapsed on the dry
earth, exhausted by the heat.

"Keep moving, Toto!" the chicks called out.
"We want to get to the lake!"

Bibi gathered them into the shade of her wings.
"We'll rest with Toto for a while," she said, "until
we are all strong enough to continue together."

While they waited, she told them about life on the lake.

Her stories of cool waters and fresh food gave Toto strength.
When he was ready, they all set off again.

"You stay beside me," Bibi told him.

On and on and on they walked,
across the scorching desert.

The shimmering outline of the volcano was slowly getting nearer, and at last they saw a sliver of silver glistening below it.

"I can see the lake!" Toto called out.

The chicks felt
damp earth beneath
their feet. Soon they
were splashing through
the cool water to join
their grateful parents.

For the rest of the summer, Bibi watched happily as the chicks grew, their feathers turning pink and readying for flight.

But she had begun to feel tired and old.

She knew that once the chicks could fly, the flock would move on. Bibi worried that she might not be strong enough to join them this time.

She slipped quietly away by herself.

Soon it was time for the flamingos to leave.

"Where is Bibi?" asked Toto.

Thousands of eyes searched the lake for their old friend.

"I see her!" Toto called. "She's lying on the shore."

The flamingos helped Bibi to stand.

"Let's clean off this sand," said one flamingo,
softly preening her feathers.

"Come back to the lake and eat with us," said another, leading her gently into the water.

"We'll all wait until you feel strong enough to fly," said Toto.

Bibi ate and rested. Slowly, slowly, she gathered her strength,
and at last she was ready.

One by one, the flamingos took to the sky, until it was Bibi's turn to try.

She whispered one last goodbye to the lake,
stretched out her wings and ran . . .

. . . and she flew!

For Cath, for Nan and for Sheila who have all walked beside me.

Published by
PEACHTREE PUBLISHING COMPANY INC.
1700 Chattahoochee Avenue
Atlanta, Georgia 30318-2112
PeachtreeBooks.com

Text and illustrations © 2022 by Jo Weaver

First published in Great Britain in 2022 by Hodder & Stoughton
First United States version published in 2023 by Peachtree Publishing
Company Inc.

Imported by Zoie Konneker

The illustrations were rendered in charcoal and digitally colored.

Printed and bound in January 2023 in China.
10 9 8 7 6 5 4 3 2 1
First Edition
ISBN: 978-1-68263-553-7

Cataloging-in-Publication Data is available from the Library of Congress.

Every few years, three-quarters of the world's lesser flamingos migrate from all over East Africa to breed on the shores of Lake Natron in Tanzania. They build their mud nests on salt islands in the middle of the lake, safely surrounded by water too caustic for predators to cross. As the water evaporates in the heat, the adults must fly to fresh water. A few adult birds stay behind to lead the chicks by foot over twenty to thirty miles (thirty to fifty kilometers) of hostile salt desert to the safety of fresh water and their parents.

Lesser flamingos feed on algae, which gives them their pink color.

The Swahili word "bibi" means "grandmother," and "toto" roughly translates to "child."